Secrets and Spies

Collect all the Magic Trix *books*

Secrets and Spies

Sara Grant

Illustrated by Erica-Jane Waters

Orion
Children's Books

First published in Great Britain in 2014
by Orion Children's Books
a division of the Orion Publishing Group Ltd
Orion House
5 Upper St Martin's Lane
London WC2H 9EA
An Hachette UK company

1 3 5 7 9 10 8 6 4 2

A catalogue record for this book is
available from the British Library.

ISBN 978 1 4440 0785 5

Printed in Great Britain by Clays Ltd, St Ives plc

To my mum, who has always
demonstrated kindness and generosity –
the true traits of a fairy godmother!

Chapter One

"Tricky Trix Morgan rockets past the defenders," Trix said in her best football commentator voice. "It's the final minute of extra time, and the title is only one kick away." Trix guided the football towards her pretend goal, which had a wooden bench and a rubbish bin for goalposts.

Trix loved to sprint as fast as her legs could go. It felt like the zing of a shooting star mixed with the sugary chill of double-fudge ice cream. It was almost as wonderful as the moment she'd discovered that she was a witch and met her magical familiar – a cheeky black and white kitten named Jinx. He was scampering beside her now and nudging the ball with his pink nose. Jinx was only visible to witches, so no one in the park could see that Trix was getting some magical help.

"Gotcha!" Oscar, Trix's pesky younger brother, dived feet first at Trix. Jinx leaped out of the way as Trix quickly swept the ball to Holly.

Oscar's feet tangled with Trix's and she fell to the grass with a thud. Holly shuffled the ball forwards. Trix had tried to tell her that she shouldn't wear a skirt, even a denim one, but Holly wouldn't give up her girly style for anyone or anything, including football. Trix knew how to dress for sports. She had tied her long wavy hair back in two bunches. She wore one black and one white trainer, which sort of matched her black and gold football kit – the strip of her favourite team, the Little

Witching Wizards.

"You can do it, Holly!" Trix cheered as she hauled Oscar to his feet, keeping one hand tightly clenched around his wrist. She didn't want Oscar to ruin Holly's only shot on goal today. He was supposed to be playing football with his own friends, not interrupting their game.

With a little help from Jinx, Holly positioned the ball and then, with her best ballerina kick, she tapped it across the goal line.

"Score!" Trix shouted. "The Holly Trixsters win the cup!" Trix released Oscar. While he chased after the ball, Trix and Holly danced their special victory dance. They swooped in a figure of eight with arms stretched wide and then hooked arms and twirled until they fell on the soft green grass, dizzy and laughing.

The sun directed its rays like a spotlight on Trix and Holly. It seemed as if everyone in Little Witching had decided to spend Sunday afternoon in the park. Clusters of friends and families circled like mini solar systems around picnic blankets, the playground and the football pitch.

Jinx came bounding over. His spots were sparkling. That's what they always did when he was happy. He curled up on Trix's chest and began to purr. Trix felt as if happiness was radiating from her.

Suddenly a round shadow zoomed across the sky. "Watch out!" Trix screamed when she realised that the incoming object was a football heading straight for them. Jinx jumped off Trix's chest as the girls rolled in opposite directions. The ball landed right between them.

"Oscar!" Trix and Holly shouted in unison.

They stood up and dusted themselves off. "Why can't you be nice for once in your life?" Trix said.

"That's no fun!" Oscar said, and placed the ball at his feet and whipped his leg back.

"Don't you dare," Trix threatened. She could see the ball was aimed right at a girl who was sitting, reading, under the biggest oak tree in the park.

"Who's going to stop me?" And, with that, Oscar let loose, sending the ball rocketing through the air.

Creeping cats!

Trix and Holly lunged for the ball. They missed and could only watch in horror as the football smashed right into the girl. Her book went flying, but she somehow managed to catch the ball.

"I'm so sorry," Trix said as she raced over. "My little brother is a pest." Oscar seemed to have disappeared. He had a talent for doing that when he'd caused trouble. Trix picked up the girl's book.

The girl had straggly black hair that stuck out in every direction. Trix couldn't tell if she hadn't brushed it or if that was her hairstyle. She wore faded blue jeans and a grey, wrinkled hoodie. Again, Trix wasn't sure if this was high fashion or just messy. Holly had shown her pictures in a glossy magazine that looked a little like the girl's outfit.

"Yeah, whatever," the girl said and snatched her book back.

"Would you like to play football with us?" Trix asked.

The girl glared at her. "What makes you think I would want to play football, with you or anybody? It's a stupid, awful game and I hate it." She grabbed a pointy stick, drove it into the football and then stormed off.

Air hissed out of the ball. Trix picked up the stick with the squashed ball on top. It looked like a very odd lollipop. This was the fourth football this month that had been lost or damaged because of Oscar. Her parents were never going to buy her another one.

But at times like this being a witch came in handy. All she needed was a sneaky quick-fix spell. "*Fix yourself and make it quick. Re-inflate when I remove this stick*," she whispered to the ball and then yanked out the stick.

With a quiet *hiss* and a slight *pop* the hole made by the stick disappeared, and the ball was round once more.

Holly's eyebrows arched in surprise. "Did you use . . ." Holly nearly said *magic* but she caught herself just in time. She wasn't supposed to know Trix was a witch. No one outside the Sisterhood of Magic was supposed to know Trix's secret. Holly had found out by accident and she was sworn to secrecy.

Oscar skidded to a stop in front of his big sister and grabbed the ball. "I thought that girl popped it!" Oscar exclaimed, rolling it around in his hands.

"Um, she . . ." Trix started but she didn't have a great explanation to cover up her use of magic.

Holly swiped the ball from Oscar and the stick from Trix. "It was an optical illusion," Holly said and moved the stick back and forth behind the ball. From where Trix and Oscar were standing, it almost looked like the stick was passing through the ball. Almost! "It's like one of my magic tricks," Holly explained. She wanted to be a magician one day, or maybe a celebrity chef, or, after today, maybe the first ballerina football superstar!

"I'm sure that ball was flat a minute ago," Oscar said, his forehead wrinkled in confusion.

"Don't be silly, Oscar." Trix tried to laugh but her chuckle sounded fake.

"Something funny is going on," Oscar said and squinted at Trix and Holly. "I'm going to find out what it is!" Oscar drop-kicked the ball and raced after it.

Trix felt as deflated as a football pierced with a stick. If Oscar discovered she was a witch, it would be worse than a sting from a bumblebee or school on Saturday or Christmas cancelled for ever.

Chapter Two

For the rest of the weekend Trix was extra careful not to be the least bit magical. She didn't cast a spell to stop Oscar when he used four of her twenty-three cat toys for target practice. She didn't magically remove the purple stain from her shirt when he spit his blackcurrant squash at her. She wanted to turn him into a slimy salamander when he chucked her favourite green glitter pen over the hedge, but she didn't.

No matter what Trix did or where she went, Oscar was always watching. On the way to school on Monday morning, he walked a few feet behind her with a tiny notebook and pen, ready to write down anything suspicious.

Trix was relieved when the school bell rang for the last lesson of the day and she could use all the magic she wanted in the magic classroom, which was hidden at the back of the Little Witching Primary School library. Every weekday, Trix and Becka from Little Witching Primary, and Stella, Pippa and Cara from the Enchanted Grove School for Girls, took lessons with Lulu the librarian on how to use their magical powers. The best and brightest witches would become fairy godmothers and Trix wanted, more than anything, to be a fairy godmother and grant wishes.

"Magic marbles!" Lulu shouted when her witchy pupils and their familiars had arrived.

Poof! A gigantic fish bowl – almost big enough to hold Trix-sized fish – appeared

in the middle of the room where Lulu's cauldron used to be. Inside the fish bowl were hundreds, maybe even thousands, of marbles. They glowed rainbow colours and sparkled like summer sunshine on a swimming pool.

"Gather round, my little witches and friendly familiars," Lulu called, waving her students forward, which set her bracelets jingle-jangling. "Today is a very special day. You will take the first step towards becoming fairy godmothers with your first wish-granting assignment!"

Trix's whole body started to tingle as if

lightning bolts were zipping through her veins. Jinx's tail began to twitch; he was excited too.

Witches and familiars crowded around the giant fish bowl, pressing their noses and beaks against the shimmering glass. Twitch, the lavender rat, scampered up the arm of his witch, Pippa, for a closer look. Cara's familiar, Tabby the cat, settled next to Jinx. Sherlock the owl perched on Becka's shoulder and hooted with excitement. Rascal, Stella's rambunctious pug, inspected the bowl from every side.

"Each marble represents a wish by someone in Little Witching," Lulu said as she circled the classroom. "The magical marbles are like mini-crystal balls. Each one will show where its Wisher is at any time."

Trix thought she saw faces reflected in each round surface. The marbles were multiplying by the minute. So many wishes! New marbles appeared with a *pop!* She wondered what people were wishing. Some greedy people wished for things they didn't need, but others made wishes about what was missing or lost or damaged in their lives. She suddenly felt very small and just a little sad when she thought of all those people in need. Trix couldn't wait to help *those* Wishers.

"I hope my Wisher wants something sparkly!" Stella piped up. *"Shimmer, glitter, sparkle, shine."* Trix immediately recognised Stella's favourite spell. *"Nothing like jewellery to make me feel fine!"* A swirl of pink glitter spun like a tornado around Stella. When it vanished, Stella was covered from head to toe in jewellery. She had a tiara that

was nearly as tall as a garden
gnome. Dozens of necklaces
were draped around her
neck. Her arms rattled
with bracelets and her ears
drooped with diamonds.
Her fingers were spread
wide with rings on each
finger.

Trix and Pippa glanced
at each other and rolled their
eyes. Stella was such a show-
off. Trix wondered if Stella
would ever be a fairy godmother.

"Granting wishes is tough stuff," Lulu
said, plucking the tiara from Stella's head and
placing it on her own. "Fast spells and quick
fixes won't help your Wisher."

With a flick of her bangle-filled wrist and
a click of her fingers, Lulu summoned a magic
wand with a star on the top. She waved it in
the air. She was writing something. Three
swirly curvy Ds appeared in glimmering
lights in front of her. "You must master the

three Ds of
wish
granting
– Discover!
Decide!
And Deliver!"

The letters morphed into
the three words as they
tripped off Lulu's tongue.
"You must *discover* all you
can about your Wisher,
decide how you can fulfil
the Wisher's secret desire,
and *deliver* the wish!"

Trix thought that didn't
sound too difficult.

"Wish granting isn't as easy as you might
think," Lulu continued as if she could read
Trix's mind. "Wishers don't always know
what's best for them. A fairy godmother
is more than just an order-taker. Fairy
godmothers must be sure that the wishes they
grant will truly bring their Wishers happiness."

"Um, miss," Stella waved her ring-filled

hand. Shiny gems twinkled in the light of the magic classroom. "I'm not sure I understand. If an ugly person wants to be pretty, surely that's an easy wish to grant. I mean, who wouldn't be happy being pretty?" Stella flipped her perfectly straightened hair. It snagged on a big crystal pendant and then twisted in her gaudy diamond rings. "Oh!" Stella squealed as she became more tangled in her jewellery.

"You are proving my point," Lulu said, with what Trix thought was a cheeky smile. "The jewellery you wished for has ended up causing you pain. Beauty shines from within. It's not applied to the outside." With a flick of Lulu's wrist and a click of her fingers, all of Stella's bling vanished.

Stella's cheeks flushed pink. She smoothed and smoothed and smoothed her hair.

"Each of you will pick one marble. Your first wish-granting task is to *discover*. Each witch should find out as much as she can about her Wisher." Lulu looked from witch to witch. "Trix, why don't you go first? Hold out your hands."

Trix did as Lulu instructed and a marble snaked from the bottom of the bowl and burst from the pile with a *swoosh*! It hovered above the fish bowl and then plopped right into Trix's hands.

The marble projected a beam of light onto the ceiling. Trix gulped as the image of her Wisher came into focus. She couldn't believe her eyes. She recognised that mess of dark hair and the nasty frown. It was the girl from the park yesterday – the one who had yelled at her and burst her football.

The witches from the Enchanted Grove School for Girls gasped.

Stella laughed. "Good luck helping her!"

Pippa whispered in Trix's ear, "She's only attended Enchanted Grove for one week and everyone already calls her Mean Melinda."

How was Trix ever going to grant the wish of the meanest girl in town?

Chapter Three

"Jinx, you are on Oscar patrol," Trix told Jinx as they left the magic classroom. "Maybe if we hurry we can meet up with Melinda at the bus stop and I can try to get to know her better. But I can't do it if Oscar's around because he'll find a way to ruin it."

Jinx nodded and marched circles around Trix as they headed down the corridor. His bright yellow eyes searched for any sign of Oscar.

Trix and Jinx met Holly at her Cookery class.

Trix told Holly about her wish-granting assignment and her plan to accidentally bump into Melinda. All the Enchanted Grove School for Girls students were picked up and dropped off at the bus stop each day. Trix was so smart; she had devised the perfect plan.

As they walked out of school, Jinx froze. He made his body as straight as an arrow, pointing his nose at one of the gateposts to Little Witching Primary School.

"What's the matter, Jinx?" Trix asked. "Oh," she sighed when she spotted Oscar peeking out and then ducking back behind the post.

"Drat and double drat," Holly said. "We must think like spies. The first thing we need to do is shake our tail."

Jinx did as she suggested and shook his long, bushy tail. He didn't know how humans lived without tails to shake and twitch and point and swish.

Trix laughed when she noticed Jinx's twitching tail. "Holly means we need to make sure Oscar doesn't follow us," Trix explained to Jinx and scratched him behind the ear. "Let's go!"

Trix set off in the wrong direction. What was his witch doing? Jinx knew that the bus stop for the Enchanted Grove School for Girls was the other way. She started to run, looping around the school and then snaking down a few side streets. Holly and Jinx tried their best to keep up.

"I think we lost him." Trix was panting by the time they reached the bus stop.

"This losing your tail stuff is more difficult than it looks in the police shows my dad watches on TV," Holly said when she caught up with Trix.

Jinx panicked. LOSING YOUR TAIL! He spun in a tight circle. Phew. His tail was still there.

Trix crouched down and smoothed Jinx's ruffled fur. "Jinx, your tail is safe. Holly was talking about Oscar. On police shows they say someone is tailing you when they mean following."

Jinx nodded, feeling relieved. Humans were very strange creatures indeed. Sometimes they seemed to talk in riddles.

Jinx patrolled the bus stop. Oh, how he loved being a spy. Cats made the best spies because of their natural spy abilities. He blinked to test his laser-like vision. He could see the Enchanted Grove School for Girls bus dead ahead. He pranced on his paws; they were ready to run. He whipped his tail in the air and pointed at the bus. Yes, his cat compass was working. He twisted his ears back and forth. He could hear rustling in the bushes behind the bus shelter. Maybe he should check it out . . .

"Here comes the bus," Trix said with a slight tremor in her voice. Jinx rushed to his witch's side. He could sense she was nervous. He'd be nervous too if he had to talk to the mean girl.

"Be yourself," Holly told Trix. "Most people won't be mean if you act kindly to them. I know you can do it!"

The Enchanted Grove School bus rolled to a stop. The first one to get off was Melinda. She pulled a wrinkled hoodie from her rucksack and slipped it over her school uniform. She tugged the hood up so that it nearly covered her face.

Jinx crept as close as he dared to Melinda. She didn't look mean, but Jinx knew that looks could be deceiving. Take Stella, for example – Stella looked nice but definitely did and said mean things sometimes. Melinda removed something from her rucksack. Jinx shrank away. Maybe it was a big stick or a water balloon or super-stinky spray. Jinx tried to imagine what other evil devices mean people kept hidden in their rucksacks.

It was a book. A book? Books weren't evil. According to Trix, books were full of amazing adventures and Jinx loved action and adventure!

Melinda smiled ever so slightly as she cracked the book open. If it wasn't for Jinx's spy vision, he

wouldn't have noticed it at all. She had a nice smile, Jinx thought. She had lovely white teeth and even a dimple when she smiled.

"Um, uh, hi," Trix said and waved at Melinda.

Melinda grunted a response which, to Jinx, sounded sort of dog-like.

"Um, Melinda," Trix started. Her hands were shaking so much that she tucked them into her blazer pockets. Jinx's whiskers were ready to wiggle if she needed an extra boost of magic – or confidence.

Melinda slammed her book shut. "You're the girl from the park yesterday."

"Um, yes. I'm sorry that my annoying little brother nearly hit you with his football. Do you have a little brother? If you do, then you'll understand . . ." Trix rambled when she got nervous.

"I know what you're trying to do and it won't work," Melinda growled.

Jinx tilted his head and squinted up at Melinda. She couldn't possibly have guessed that Trix was a witch-in-training on her first wish-granting assignment. Maybe Melinda was talking about something else. Humans were very confusing sometimes.

Now everyone at the bus stop was staring at Trix and Melinda, including Stella and the other witches from the Enchanted Grove School for Girls, who had all piled off the bus. Trix opened her mouth, but nothing came out. It was as if she had become a human ice sculpture.

"Just leave me alone!" Melinda snapped. Then she flipped open her book and walked away. Jinx thought she must be pretty smart to be able to walk and read at the same time.

"Great job as a fairy godmother," Stella muttered to Trix as she pushed past. Jinx knew that she meant exactly the opposite of what she'd said. "You might as well turn in your broom."

Ooo, Stella was so mean! Jinx hated how her words could sting like nettles. Jinx wished he could make Trix feel better because, if he was honest, he thought getting to know Melinda was going to be more dangerous than cuddling a boa constrictor.

Chapter Four

The next day the magic classroom was buzzing. The witches were chattering and the familiars were meowing, barking, hooting and squeaking with delight.

"Magic up, my little witches." The air around Lulu shimmered as if she had a halo of glitter. "Who can tell me the three Ds of wish granting?"

All the girls raised their hands. Lulu

pointed to Trix.

"Discover, decide and deliver," Trix answered. She knew the correct answer even if she hadn't *discovered* anything about Melinda. Trix silently wished as hard as she could that Lulu wouldn't ask her about Melinda. She didn't want to disappoint Lulu or embarrass herself in front of the other witches.

"That's right, Trix," Lulu said. "Does anyone want to share what they've discovered?"

Pippa's hand shot up. She rose on her tippy toes. Her high ponytail swished with excitement and she started speaking before Lulu even had a chance to call on her.

"My Wisher's name is Gladys Eugenie Victoria Alexandra Cumberbatch. She owns the Chat Noir Café, which means the Black Cat Café, on the high street. She's seventy-eight years old. She was never married and has no children. Her favourite colour is violet. She loves to bake tea cakes . . ." On and on Pippa went. She knew practically every detail of Gladys' life.

Trix shrank behind the other witches. She felt a complete and utter failure as a fairy godmother so far.

"Wow, Pippa!" Lulu said when Pippa paused to take a breath. "Magically marvellous!"

"I'm not finished. Gladys likes to watch black and white movies, and — "

"That's wonderful," Lulu interrupted Pippa, "but let's give someone else a chance. "How about . . ." Lulu looked at each of her pupils.

Trix studied her trainers. *Please, oh, please, oh, please don't call on me,* she thought.

"Becka," Lulu said. Trix let out a sigh of relief.

Becka twirled the curl at the end of her plait around and around her finger. "Well, my Wisher's name is Zack Sergeant." Becka blushed. "He's in Year Eleven. He plays rugby."

"And he's really cute," Stella put in, nudging Becka with her elbow.

Becka held up her magic marble and the image of a boy with wavy dark hair and big brown eyes was projected onto the wall of the magic classroom. Trix had to agree that he was pretty handsome. Why hadn't she got someone like Zack? Why did she have to pick Mean Melinda?

When Becka had finished talking, Lulu whirled around and set her bracelets jingle-jangling. "Today you will focus on the second D – *decide*! Can anyone tell me what that means?"

Cara stepped forwards. "You have to decide how you can fulfil the wish," she said.

Lulu nodded. "That's correct! But it's not as straightforward as it sounds. You've heard the saying: *Be careful what you wish for*?" Lulu smiled at Trix. "Can you explain what I mean by that, Trix?"

Trix understood exactly what Lulu meant. "When I was much younger, I wished and wished for a baby brother. Then I got one." She'd wanted a baby to play with and dress up, but it had turned out that babies weren't so much fun – especially when the baby was Oscar. "Oscar has been a number one pest since the day he was born," Trix said, and then blushed because that sounded mean. "I love him but he's a brat," she added.

"Oh, I understand!" Pippa exclaimed. "We have to figure out *why* they want what they want, because giving them what they ask for may not get them what they really need." Pippa giggled. "Or something like that."

Trix's forehead crinkled in confusion as she tried to sort out the point that Pippa was trying to make.

"You've got the right idea," Lulu said and then she closed her eyes. Trix could tell Lulu was thinking because a glittery light bulb appeared over Lulu's head.

When Lulu's eyelids sprang open, the light bulb burst in a shower of sparkles that rained down over the girls. "Let me see if I can explain it a bit more clearly. Some people wish for *things* but things don't often make them feel better. You have to use your human powers of listening and problem-solving before you use your magic. So listen and learn and try to uncover what your Wisher *really* needs – not what they think they want. Got it?" The girls all nodded. "I know you can do it!"

Trix felt encouraged by Lulu's lesson. She *could* do it – even if she was behind all the other witches in her wish-granting assignment. Football teams often came from behind and won matches. But then she thought of Oscar the super snoop, and remembered how mean Melinda had been when Trix had tried to talk to her. Being a fairy godmother was going to take brains, imagination and, in Trix's case, a miracle!

Chapter Five

Trix's magic marble flashed a rainbow of colours as it projected an image of Melinda on the ceiling of Trix's bedroom. Trix, Holly and Jinx had raced home after school so Trix could get right to work on her wish-granting assignment. Jinx sat nearly camouflaged among Trix's twenty-three toy cats.

"That's super-duper amazing," Holly said, transfixed by the magic marble. "So that's

Melinda right now. This is like watching a reality TV show."

"The image fades away sometimes," Trix said. "It seems to know when the Wisher wants privacy."

Holly's eyes flicked left and right. "What if someone is watching us right now? It's kind of weird. Being a fairy godmother is a big responsibility, isn't it?"

Trix nodded. She felt the weight of it. Being magical brought so many wonderful possibilities, but if she was to become a fairy godmother then she had a job to do!

"I have to discover as much as I can about her and then I have to decide how to fulfil her *true* desire," Trix said. It was like solving a riddle and taking a test all jumbled together.

Trix and Holly studied Melinda. Her nose was buried in a book, and yet she was walking around with someone else who was always out of view.

"I think she's at a shopping centre," Holly said as the names of clothing stores flashed by. "I wish I was shopping! Oh, look at that cute dress." Holly pointed as Melinda shuffled past a green dress that would look gorgeous on Holly with her curly red hair. "Wait! Go back. Was that a sale?" Holly picked up the marble and shook it. "How do we rewind?"

Trix took the marble and placed it back on her bed. "It doesn't work like that. We can only see what's happening right now."

Someone was showing Melinda pillowcases and duvet covers now. Melinda would glance up from her book from time to time, shake her head and return to reading.

"They must be shopping for stuff for Melinda's new bedroom," Trix said.

"I wish I could redecorate my room," Holly said, rearranging the pillows and toys on Trix's bed. "My colours would be fuchsia and rose."

"You mean pink and pink," Trix laughed. It would never occur to Trix to have a colour scheme for her bedroom. She loved that they were so different and yet still best friends. They were puzzle pieces that fit perfectly. What would she do without Holly? "What do you think Melinda needs?"

"I've got it!" Holly sprang to her feet. "The girl needs a makeover!"

That didn't seem quite right to Trix, but she didn't have any better ideas. Melinda did look as if she'd dressed in the dark. She was wearing a purple hoodie with what may have been a few tea stains down the front.

"Practise on me!" Holly bounced up and down on Trix's bed, sending Jinx and Trix's toy cats wiggling and jiggling.

Trix screwed up her face, thinking. She

decided to borrow a spell from the queen of mean – and makeovers – Stella. "*Shimmer, glimmer, nails, make-up and hair. Give us something amazing to wear!*"

Trix's room filled with a glittering cloud. Trix couldn't see anything but twinkling lights. She felt as if a thousand flower petals were tickling her. She could hear Holly's giggle-snort of laughter. When the wispy cloud cleared, Holly gasped.

Jinx leaped to the floor. His back arched. His tail pointed straight up, and he hissed at the pair.

"It's OK, Jinx," Trix cooed. "It's just Holly and me." But they didn't look like Trix and Holly any more. Trix's spell had transformed them both into circus clowns!

Their hair was teased out into round balls. Trix's hair was rainbow striped, while Holly's was bright pink. Their faces were covered with thick white makeup and huge red smiles were painted around their mouths. Even their eyelids were streaked with bright blue and green eyeshadow and they were dressed in

colourful, baggy jumpsuits with wide, white
ruffles at their necks, wrists and ankles.

"Some makeover!" Holly reached out and
honked the red ball on Trix's nose.

Trix couldn't believe how terribly wrong
her makeover spell had gone.

Her bedroom door banged open. "Can't
you two weirdoes . . ." Oscar's words faded
away as he caught sight of his sister and her
best friend.

Trix had to think fast. "Holly and I are trying
out costumes for Halloween," she told him.

"But Halloween's not for ages," Oscar replied.

"You should not come into my room without knocking, anyway," Trix said and shoved Oscar back out onto the landing before shutting the door.

"Change us back, right now," Holly said, tapping her oversized red clown shoe.

Trix thought for a second before she cast her un-makeover spell. *"No more costumes. This I can fix. Please turn us back to Holly and Trix!"*

A chilly blast of air swept over them and Trix and Holly looked like themselves again.

Oscar barged into the room again, this time with a camera in his hand. The camera flashed. "I'm going to put this picture on the Internet so the world can see how weird you both . . ." Oscar looked at the camera's digital display and then stared up at the girls in amazement.

"How did you change so fast?" he asked.

"We, um . . ." Trix started, but she had no idea how to finish the sentence.

"Don't tell me it's another opti-whatever illusion." Oscar planted his fists on his hips. "That's just another word for magic. And magic's the only way you could have changed so fast." Oscar's eyes widened in surprise and realisation. "That's it, isn't it?"

"No, of course not. There's no such thing as magic," Holly said, laughing nervously. "You remember when I performed magic at the talent show. It was all just a trick."

"Yes! We were playing a trick on you, Oscar," Trix tried to explain, but her secret was like a cauldron boiling over with potions. It bubbled inside her. She felt as if her magic was sneaking out from her fingers and toes and eyes and nose. Keeping a super-duper secret was difficult.

"There *is so* magic," Oscar said, stamping his foot. "And one of you two knows how to do it and I'm going to find out who and then I'm going to tell the world!" Oscar stormed out, slamming the door behind him.

Trix felt really worried. How was she ever going to prove Oscar wrong, when he was absolutely right?

Chapter Six

The next day as Trix entered the magic classroom, her stomach felt as if it had been stretched like a rubber band, tied in a knot and curled like the twirly ribbons on top of birthday presents. Not only was she no closer to granting Melinda's wish or even knowing what Melinda thought she wanted, but Oscar was watching her and Holly's every move. He kept popping up – from behind the sofa or the bushes in their front garden – and snapping photos.

What was Lulu saying?

Trix couldn't concentrate in school and now she realised she'd missed half of Lulu's lesson.

"Things have changed since the early days when the first fairy godmother granted Cinderella's wish with lots of amazing magic," Lulu said and pointed to a wedding portrait of Cinderella and her Prince Charming. "Because your Wisher lives in Little Witching, you must grant the wish *secretly*. Any magic must appear to come about through normal circumstances." Lulu sighed. "I must admit, sometimes I miss the good old days."

"I thought it would be like in the movies," Stella whined. "You know, we wear a glamorous ballgown and wave a wand."

"Sorry, Stella, but for now your wish granting – just like the fact that you are a witch – must remain a secret." Then Lulu paused as she studied her witches-in-training. "But if you work really hard and are promoted to a fairy godmother then sometimes, when you are granting wishes in far-away places, you may get to dress up as traditional fairy godmothers and grant a few special wishes."

Trix shifted so she was standing behind the other witches. At this rate she was never going to become a real fairy godmother. She wished she could disappear. Jinx brushed against her leg. Then, in a blink, he was in her arms. His spots sparkled. He was trying to comfort her. She stroked his soft fur and felt the tickle of his purrs. He did make her feel a bit better. She held him close. "Thanks, Jinx."

"The best way to teach you the third and final D – deliver – is to show you," Lulu said and gestured to Cara. "Cara has agreed to let us watch her grant her Wisher's wish. For this, it's better not to be there."

What?

Lulu gathered the witches and familiars and recited a very long spell that included the words *invisible* and *transportation*. Trix marvelled at Lulu's amazing rhyming skill.

In a flash, they were transported to the Little Witching Riding School. Jinx jumped from Trix's arms and raced Rascal and the other familiars to the nearby meadow. Cara was now dressed in her riding clothes – black boots, a tan jacket and a riding hat – but Lulu and the other witches were transparent. Trix waved her hands in front of her face. She could see right through them!

Lulu stepped next to Trix. "Don't worry," she said. "We can see each other but no one else can see us."

"This is really cool!" Pippa exclaimed, spinning with outstretched arms. A nearby horse whinnied and galloped away. "Oh, sorry," Pippa called to the horse.

"We may not be seen, but we can still be heard," Lulu explained. "And animals can sense our presence so we need to keep still. Cara, can you tell us a little about your Wisher?"

Cara smoothed her ponytail which poked out from beneath her hat. "Her name is Julia and she has been very sad. She used to live on a farm until her dad lost his job in the city. After that, she and her family had to move into a flat that doesn't allow any animals."

Trix could sympathise. She had always wanted a kitten but her dad was allergic to cats. She could only have Jinx because Lulu had made him invisible, and Trix kept Jinx and her dad away from each other.

Cara whispered to her audience of invisible

witches, "I've been helping out at the stables so I could get to know Julia better. She wishes she had her old life again, but I couldn't give her dad his job back, or anything like that, so I had to think of something else. I think Julia is really missing having a pet. We all know how lovely it is to have our familiars," Cara glanced at the two cats, pug, rat and owl all tumbling happily about in the meadow, "so I had an idea for how I could give her a furry companion. The owners of the riding school are witches too, so I had a little help. Well, you'll see what I mean. Here she comes . . ."

"Let the magic begin!" Lulu swept them a few steps away from Cara.

"Hi, Julia!" Cara called and waved to a girl Trix recognised from school. She was a few years older than Trix.

"Hi, Cara," Julia said as she walked over to a paddock where several horses were grazing. She clicked her tongue and whistled. One chestnut and another black horse trotted towards her.

"You're good with animals," Cara said and

joined Julia, who was stroking the white star on the nose of the chestnut. "This is Starlight," she continued. "He just moved into the stables. His owners are pensioners. They're moving to Spain." Cara patted the horse's nose. "The stable owners have asked me if I know anyone who would like to help with Starlight. They're looking for someone to ride him and take care of him. You know . . ." Cara glanced over at Julia, "someone to sort of *adopt* him."

"I could do that!" Julia said eagerly. Starlight shook his mane as if he were happy too. Julia rubbed noses with the horse. Starlight appeared to lean into Julia as if they were meant to be together. When Julia pulled away from him, tears were streaming down her face. "This is a dream come true," she said softly.

Trix felt a rush of happiness for Julia. Watching the girl's wish being granted made Trix feel as if she was also receiving an extraordinary gift. She let out a little squeak of excitement.

"Did you hear something?" Julia asked.

Lulu placed a finger to her lips, reminding the girls to be quiet.

"Let's go and work out all the details," Cara said quickly, leading Julia over to the office.

When Cara and Julia were far enough away, Lulu huddled the other witches together. "Cara thought everything through and was able to grant Julia's wish even though Julia herself didn't realise that this was what she needed. So now it's your turn. Remember the three Ds but don't forget the big E," Lulu smiled her biggest smile. "Enjoy! Don't forget to have fun. I can't wait to hear about your amazing wish granting!"

And with that Trix felt the rush of magical transportation as Lulu swept them back to the magic classroom. Trix vowed to try again with Melinda. She wanted to feel that wonderful rush of happiness that came with helping someone's dream come true.

Chapter Seven

Jinx opened one eye and then the other. He rolled on his back and stretched one paw and then another. He wriggled in the sunlight slanting across Trix's bed. He loved an afternoon nap.

He perked up and looked out of the window. He could see Trix and Holly across the road in Holly's bedroom. They were planning a top-secret mission and Jinx wished he could go along, but he'd promised Trix he'd stay put. Last time he'd made an uninvited trip to Holly's house he had played hide and seek with Holly's guinea pig, Fuzzy-Wuzzle-Be, and they had accidentally tracked blue paint through the lounge. Jinx thought he and Fuzzy had created a wonderful painting, but Trix hadn't been too pleased.

Jinx pressed a paw on the window and wished he could be with Trix, but he was a cat of his word! The setting sun shifted lower in the sky and cast a thin beam of light under Trix's desk. Something flashed. Jinx jumped down to inspect the shiny object.

It was Trix's magic marble. Jinx batted at the marble. He loved the way it reflected polka dots of light on the walls and ceiling. Jinx chased the marble around the room. He was so dazzled by

the marble he almost didn't hear the door creaking open. Just in time, Jinx dived under Trix's bed. The magic marble rolled away and stopped near Oscar's feet. But Oscar didn't seem to notice. Instead he began to search Trix's room. He peeked in Trix's wardrobe, rummaged through her chest of drawers and looked under each of her twenty-three toy cats.

Oscar should not be snooping in Trix's room, Jinx thought. His spots burned with frustration.

What good was being a magical familiar if you couldn't use your magic to help your witch? But he had promised Trix that he would stay out of trouble. Jinx tucked himself behind the stray sock, crumpled wad of paper and broken purple brolly that lay, abandoned, under Trix's bed.

"There's got to be something in here that proves Trix and Holly are magical," Oscar muttered to himself and lay flat on the floor. Jinx scampered backwards as Oscar reached his hand under Trix's bed. Suddenly, Jinx had an idea for how he could discourage Oscar's snooping!

When Oscar's hand closed around the sock, Jinx licked his fingers with a flick of his rough pink tongue.

"Aw, yuck!" Oscar yelled as he jerked his hand back and inspected the wet patch. But unfortunately that didn't stop his snooping.

Oscar searched high and low. Jinx thought about hissing or pouncing but that would only make Oscar more suspicious of Trix. A promise is a promise! Jinx told himself.

Just as Oscar was about to leave, he spotted the glimmering magic marble.

Oh, no! Jinx thought and sprang to his feet.

"What's this?" Oscar asked, picking up the marble. He turned it over and over in his hands. "Thanks, Trix," Oscar said and, to Jinx's horror, he stuffed the marble in his pocket! "That's another marble for my collection."

Jinx knew he had to get that marble back. Jinx Super Spy to the rescue! He scampered after Oscar and slid into Oscar's room right before the door closed with a slam, nearly pinching Jinx's tail.

Oscar dropped the magic marble, with a click and a clack, into a jam jar full of marbles. Then he scrambled onto a chair and pulled a pair of binoculars from the top shelf over his desk, bringing two plastic dinosaurs, a comic book and a shower of dust down in the process. He trained the binoculars out of the window.

"Gotcha!" Oscar yelled.

What had Oscar spotted? Jinx bounced up on his hind legs trying to see.

Boing! Boing!

With each jump, he could just peep out of the window. A few more jumps and he knew what Oscar was finding so interesting – Trix and

Holly were sneaking out of Holly's house. Oscar exchanged his binoculars for a camera and raced out of his room.

Jinx dashed to the bedroom door then back to the window. Trix and Holly hadn't noticed Oscar following them and if Oscar took a photo of Trix doing something magical, then Trix would be in big trouble. Jinx needed to warn Trix but he also needed to retrieve the magic marble. He dived for the jar of marbles but then leaped onto the windowsill. He didn't know what to do first. Jinx hopped from jar to window to door. Then he paused.

What would Lulu do? he asked himself.

Lulu would slow down and do one thing at a time, he thought. So that's what Jinx did.

First he dipped his paw in the jam jar full of marbles. He loved the tappity-tap sound they made when he stirred the marbles in the jar. He rolled them all around until the magic one was at the very top of the pile. Then he extended his claws and cupped the magic marble in his paw. Gotcha!

He returned the magic marble to Trix's room. All he had to do now was use his super spy skills to warn Trix about her . . . what had Holly called it? . . . her tail! That was it. Jinx had to warn Trix and Holly that Oscar was tailing them. There was no time to lose!

Chapter Eight

"Are you sure it will work?" Holly asked as she and Trix ducked behind the overgrown rose bush at the end of their street.

"I'm never sure my magic will work the way I want it to, but let's give it a go." Trix's cheeks flushed with excitement.

"No, I mean, I'm not sure spying on Melinda is the right thing to do," Holly said.

"I've tried to be nice, haven't I?" Trix

asked. "But if she won't even talk to me, how will I ever find out what her wish is? Maybe if we study her in her . . ." *What do they say on all those nature TV shows?* Searching for the right words in Trix's brain was like fishing for a pound coin among the sofa cushions. Sometimes she found a coin but sometimes all she got was a handful of fuzz. Trix thought harder and then she remembered the words. "If we study her in her *natural habitat* then maybe we can discover why she is grumpy all the time." Trix nodded at her smart thinking, even though a tiny part of her tummy was telling her that spying wasn't very nice.

Trix opened the shopping bag she'd been carrying and showed Holly what was inside: two pairs of her mum's sunglasses and two coats that looked a little bit like the raincoats private investigators wore in old films – except one had flowers all over it and the other was bright orange with a hood.

"What do we need the raincoats for? It's not raining," Holly said, looking up at the cloudless sky.

Trix handed a pair of sunglasses and the flowery raincoat to Holly. "These are our spy disguises. Spying is the way forward. Operation Melinda's Wish is go!"

The girls dressed in their spy disguises. "I'm not sure this is going to work," Holly said, slipping the sunglasses down her nose and peering over the frames at Trix. "We sort of stand out, don't you think?"

"It works in the films." Trix flipped up the collar on Holly's coat and pulled up her hood. "First, we need to find out where Melinda lives. Here goes . . ." Trix concentrated on Melinda and cast a spell. *"Help us find Melinda. Give us a sign. Please show us the way with a sparkling line."*

A path of glowing pebbles appeared ahead of them.

"They look like glittery breadcrumbs," Holly said.

As they reached each stone, it vanished and another appeared up ahead. The girls bolted from hiding place to hiding place. They ducked behind post boxes, dived behind cars and crouched behind trees.

"Can this be right?" Holly said when the
trail ended at the entrance to the biggest
house in Little Witching. It had four big
windows on the bottom floor, five windows
on the next floor and even a few round
windows on the tippy-top floor. The front
drive was lined with trees and decorative
lanterns. "Melinda lives here?"

Trix shrugged. If her magic had worked,
then yes.

Something was glowing in the tree
nearest the house – was it the final glittery

breadcrumb? Trix grabbed Holly's hand and they crept from tree to tree until they were standing under the one where a light was bouncing from branch to branch.

"Jinx!" Trix exclaimed when her sparkling familiar came into focus. "What are you doing here?"

Jinx poked a paw in the air and his tail lashed angrily.

"I don't think Jinx likes the fact that we went spying without him," Trix said. Now that they were practically on Melinda's doorstep, Trix was starting to wonder if Operation Melinda's Wish was such a good idea.

She glanced up at the beautiful house. She was fairly sure she could see a Melinda-and-book-shaped shadow in one of the big windows upstairs. Trix's feet seemed to have an overwhelming urge to run, but Trix stayed put.

"You stand guard and do your bird whistle if someone is coming," Trix whispered to Holly, positioning her right by the tree that stood closest to Melinda's house.

Jinx jumped down and began to race

around Trix in circles. What was the matter with her crazy kitten?

"It will be fine, Jinx," Trix said, but her tummy felt as though it were full of creepy-crawly spiders and wriggly worms. She wasn't sure if she was more scared of getting caught or of failing her first fairy godmotherly mission. Trix screwed her eyes shut and tried to think of a rhyme that would help her peek in Melinda's bedroom window.

"*Lighter than air. Let me float high. Up at her window, allow me to spy,*" Trix chanted her spell. When she opened her eyes, she was floating upwards like a helium balloon.

"Creeping cats!" Trix wiggled her toes and stifled a giggle. Floating was almost as much fun as flying on her witch's broom.

Down below, she could see Jinx feverishly shaking his head. Was he trying to tell her something? Maybe he didn't like her spying, but it would only be for a few minutes and it was only so that she could help Melinda.

As she drew close to Melinda's window, she stretched out like a star to stop herself from floating higher. Then she leaned forwards and inched closer, trying to peep in from the side of the window so that Melinda wouldn't see her.

Melinda was curled up on her bed, propped up against a mountain of white fluffy pillows, with an open book right in front of her face.

Books were piled on her bedside cabinet and
stacked on a bookcase that filled one wall.
Her room was painted a bright blue and
she had a duvet cover that was patterned to
look like a cloud-filled sky. Trix's house was
decorated with knick-knacks given to her by
her grannies and bits and bobs collected from
car boot sales, but Melinda's room could have
appeared as the *after* shot in one of those
home makeover shows. Even the birds near
Melinda's house seem to chirp a perfect tune.

Trix wobbled in the air as she realised that
one particular tweet was not coming from
a bird at all! That whistle was from her best
friend Holly – and it was the signal that
someone was coming!

Chapter Nine

Trix pushed away from the house but, as she did, she lost her balance and began to spin in the air as if she were somersaulting over the bar of a climbing frame. The spinning was making her feel sick. She spread out her arms and legs, which made her stop – only she was upside down! Gently, she tucked herself into a ball and slowly turned right-side up.

Holly was whistling non-stop now and Jinx had raced from Holly's side and was pointing his paw at a small figure that stood in the shadow of a nearby tree. Trix felt sick again, but not from spinning, this time.

Oscar! At least, she was fairly sure it was him. He was wearing one of their dad's old macs and one of his hats with a brim. The hat was tipping forwards over Oscar's eyes and the coat was dragging on the ground. Seeing Oscar while she was suspended in mid-air was worse than spotting a flesh-eating zombie! She could only hope that he hadn't noticed her yet.

Desperately, she tried to think of a rhyme to reverse her floating spell. She was drifting closer to the tree. That gave her an idea – if she made it to the tree, maybe she could pretend that she'd climbed it! She grabbed a leaf and tried to pull herself closer. The leaf snapped free and Trix drifted a little higher. She kicked her legs and waved her arms as if she were swimming. It worked. Gradually, she floated close enough to the tree that she could wrap her arms around it – but her legs kept floating up, up, up!

Trix murmured, "*I don't like floating. I'm turned around. I'd like to be back down on the ground!*"

Oscar stumbled from his hiding place.

"Arghhhh!" Trix screamed as she went crashing down through the tree. She grabbed at the last branch and managed to hang on so that she was swinging from it like a monkey.

"Gotcha!" Oscar shouted as he fumbled with something under the long sleeves of Dad's coat. He held up a camera, just as Trix's arms gave out and she tumbled on top of him.

Holly raced over and helped them both to their feet.

"I saw you! You were flying!" Oscar shouted and then he paused. Trix could almost see his brain whirring as he put the pieces of the puzzle together. "And I heard you saying a rhyme. I bet you were casting a spell! You're a witch!" Oscar pointed his finger at Trix and jumped up and down with the excitement of his discovery. Then his hat slipped down over his eyes and he got so tangled in the oversized coat that he fell over again, but that didn't stop him. "I'm going to tell Mum and Dad and the police and maybe even the Prime Minister! We're going to be on TV. I might even get my own reality TV show . . ." On and on he went, listing all the ways he was going to ruin Trix's life for ever.

"Please be quiet, Oscar," Trix hissed. She glanced at Melinda's window. The curtains were twitching as if someone had just peeked out. Had Melinda seen her too?

Oh, everything was going terribly wrong!

"We need to get out of here," Trix said. She

grabbed one of Oscar's arms, Holly grabbed the other and they started to pull Oscar away from the house. But Oscar dragged his heels, making it as difficult as possible for them. And all the time he was babbling, "Trix is a witch. Trix is a witch," over and over and over again.

Think, brain, think! Trix told herself. There must be a magical way out of this mess.

They managed to get Oscar up the driveway and out of sight when Trix heard the front door of Melinda's house bang open. "You'd better leave or I'll call the police!" someone yelled. Trix didn't dare look back now.

And then an idea exploded in her mind like a firework. "I need some help, Jinx," Trix whispered to her familiar who was bounding along behind them.

"What is a Jinx?" Oscar asked, still struggling against them.

"Hold on," Trix told Holly, wrapping her brother and her best friend in an enormous bear hug. "*Rock-a-bye. Rock-a-bye. Slumber and snore. Snuggle in bed and worry no more,"* Trix recited the spell that Lulu had once used to transport her back to her own bed. Jinx wiggled his whiskers and . . .

WHOOSH!

The next moment, Oscar was tucked safely in his bed, sound asleep. Holly and Jinx ducked out of sight as Oscar mumbled, "Trix. Witch."

"There, there, little brother," Trix singsonged as she removed his hat and coat. "You are having a bad dream."

Oscar stirred. "No," he muttered. "I saw you. You were floating . . ."

"It was just a nightmare, Oscar," Trix said and tucked the duvet around him. "It was all a dream."

When Oscar started to snore, Trix, Holly and Jinx tiptoed out of his room.

"I guess I can't be mad at Oscar for spying on us when we were spying on Melinda," Trix said, a knot tightening in her tummy. "That was close."

"*Too* close," Holly replied.

Meow! Jinx agreed.

Chapter Ten

"Magic up, my lovely little witches and frightfully friendly familiars." Lulu's voice filled the magic classroom. The room began to glow and coloured lights flashed. Music filled the room. It was that rocky sort of music that always made Trix want to dance. Jinx, Twitch, Tabby, Rascal and Sherlock bopped around the room.

Something amazing was going to happen. Trix could feel it.

"Today is a very special day!" Lulu said as she magically appeared in the centre of the room. She wasn't dressed in her normal black gown. Today she wore a dazzling white dress and witch's hat that reflected the colours swirling around the magic classroom. The girls formed a circle with Lulu in the middle.

"I have been instructed by the Sisterhood of Magic to present a lovely surprise to the four witches who have granted their first wishes!" Lulu said, pointing to each girl. Silvery sashes draped themselves across the young witches' bodies.

Trix's sash already had a pink gem shimmering on it. Reflected in the shiny surface was an image of Holly. Trix had received it for helping her best friend overcome her shyness at the school's talent show. She remembered how proud she'd felt when Lulu had placed the stone there.

"Congratulations, my lovely witches! It is
my honour and duty to present these magical
jewels to you . . ." Lulu touched a point on
every sash – except Trix's – and a crystal blue
gem magically appeared.

Jinx nuzzled Trix's shoes but even a
sparkling spotted kitten wasn't going to make
her feel any better. It was official. She had
failed as a fairy godmother. But she would
try not to let herself focus on her sadness.
Trix was happy for the other witches. She
really was. She went to inspect Pippa's shiny

new award. "Well done," Trix said.

Stella polished her gem. She knocked into Trix's shoulder and said, "I'm sure you'll grant Melinda's wish one day."

Stella's mean words hurt more than they usually did.

For the rest of the class, each girl – except Trix – took turns recounting how they had granted their wishes. Trix rolled her magic marble over and over in her pocket. She hoped she looked happy and pleased for the other girls, but inside she felt stormy and dark.

When the lesson was over, Trix waited until everyone had left.

"Here!" Trix handed her magic marble to Lulu. "You'd better let a real fairy godmother grant Melinda's wish." The marble glowed and sparkled. An image of a grim-faced Melinda was projected on the wall of the magic classroom.

Lulu closed her hand around Trix's. "Fairy godmothers and their Wishers are connected. You were given Melinda for a reason. I've

faith that you will find a way to grant Melinda's wish."

"Maybe I need a special potion or an enchanted charm or something to make Melinda nice," Trix said as she tucked her magic marble back into her blazer pocket.

"A Niceness Potion would help Melinda behave nicely for a short time," Lulu explained, "but your job is to find out why Melinda is so unhappy. There's a wish – and a nice person – hiding under all that meanness."

Trix knew in her heart that Lulu was right. Like a great archaeologist who finds treasure by digging in dusty old ruins, Trix would have to discover the niceness that Melinda had buried deep, deep down inside.

Chapter Eleven

Jinx turned his spots up to maximum sparkle.
Then he danced a jig while meowing the theme
tune to Trix's favourite cartoon. Jinx and Trix
were hidden away in Trix's bedroom. When his
dance didn't make Trix smile, he snuggled up on
Trix's lap and struck his cutest pose. He batted his
golden eyes. He purred until he thought he might
burst.

Nothing!

Trix gave Jinx a stroke on his back, but not in the place she knew was his favourite. Ever since she'd got home from school, she hadn't laughed or smiled. She just lay on her bed, rolling the magic marble over and over in her hands. Images of Melinda flashed across the ceiling, the wall, the floor and even Jinx's fur.

"I am never going to be a fairy godmother if I don't think of a way to get to know Melinda," Trix moaned and buried her head under her mountain of soft toy cats.

Shuffle.

Muffle.

Thud!

The sounds were coming from downstairs. Jinx scampered over and stared at the door. He wished he had X-ray vision so he could see what was making all that noise. Was it a burglar? A swamp monster? A giant robot? Trix didn't even sit up. Why wasn't she curious?

Thump!

Bump!

Clunk!

Jinx cocked his head and pricked up his ears. He

couldn't take it any more. Trix would understand.
He had to investigate. He used his magic to pop
outside Trix's bedroom – and couldn't believe his
eyes. There was a huge chocolate bar right in front
of Trix's door. Maybe Holly or Trix's parents knew
she was feeling low and had left her a treat to cheer
her up. Jinx would take it to Trix.

But when he clawed at the wrapper, the strangest
thing happened. The bar of chocolate went flying
down the hall. Was it enchanted?

Jinx raced after it. The chocolate bar teetered
at the top of the stairs. He pounced. And now he
was zooming down the stairs on a chocolate
sledge!

Wheeeee!

The bar landed with a thump on the bottom stair. And that's when Jinx spotted it – transparent fishing wire was taped to the bottom of the chocolate bar. The chocolate wasn't enchanted. Someone was pulling the chocolate towards the lounge, reeling Jinx in like a fish on a hook.

"Gotcha!" Oscar shouted and the phone in his hand flashed.

"What's going on?" Dad shouted from the kitchen.

"Nothing!" Oscar shouted back.

Jinx leaped off the chocolate bar as Oscar snatched it up, looking bemused. "I'm sure I felt a tug. Trix can never resist chocolate! Why didn't this work?" he asked himself. He dragged a chair over to the doorway of the lounge. Jinx couldn't see exactly what he was doing but Oscar seemed to have rigged something over the door. Then Oscar jumped down and checked the tape that secured another length of fishing wire across the doorway at ankle height. "Oh, I almost forgot the best part!" he muttered, and dumped his jar full of marbles all over the floor.

That's dangerous, Jinx thought.

Oscar stamped up the stairs with the chocolate bar in his hand, trailing the wire behind him.

"What are you doing?" Mum yelled from her bedroom.

"Nothing!" Oscar called back.

But Jinx finally understood what Oscar was up to, and it was far from nothing.

Oscar was trying to lure Trix out of her room with chocolate and draw her to the lounge where she would trip over the marbles, stumble into the wire and trigger whatever Oscar had placed overhead to come crashing down on top of her. It was a Trix trap!

Jinx batted the marbles away, clearing a path for Trix. Then he hopped from the back of the sofa to the bookcase. From here he could see a dozen wibbly-wobbly balloons balanced over the door to the lounge. Water balloons!

Why had Oscar gone to so much trouble? He was always a pest but this was super-duper mean, even for him.

Oscar came hopping down the stairs with a loud thump! Thump! THUMP!

"Oscar!" Dad yelled from the kitchen.

"Oscar!" Mum echoed from upstairs.

"I'M NOT DOING ANYTHING!" Oscar replied at maximum volume. He tiptoed into the lounge, carefully stepping over his trip wire. He re-scattered the marbles and positioned himself in the centre of the room, holding the string attached to the chocolate bar in one hand and Mum's phone in the other.

"Oh, Tri-ix!" Oscar called sweetly. "I've got a surprise for you!"

"Buzz off, Oscar!" Trix yelled from upstairs, but Jinx heard Trix's bedroom door creak open. The string in Oscar's hand was pulled tight.

Jinx knew he had to do something or Trix would be caught in Oscar's trap. He dived for the wire that was attached to the chocolate bar. He only meant to pull it away, but his claw got caught and suddenly Jinx was tangled in the wire and tumbling over the marbles. He was rolling straight for the trip wire. He felt the wire give. With a WHOOSH the balloons burst, splattering him with water. Jinx untangled himself and shook from the top of his nose to the tip of his tail, spraying water everywhere.

"What's that?" Oscar gasped.

A red light was blinking on the phone in Oscar's hand. Oscar was filming! Maybe he couldn't see Jinx exactly but the water might be creating a shiny Jinx outline that would show up on camera! Jinx panicked but, before he could do anything, Trix appeared.

"Oscar!" Trix shouted, bursting into the room. Then she screamed as she tripped on the marbles, slipped on the water and stumbled into the bookcase. Mum's favourite purple sculpture toppled from the top shelf.

Jinx jumped over Trix and dived for the sculpture. Paws outstretched, he caught the sculpture mid-air but it slipped on his wet fur and . . .

CRASH!

Purple shards of glass rained down on the lounge as the sculpture shattered into a million pieces.

Jinx heard Trix murmur, "Why did Mum's sculpture have to smash? I need to fix it in a flash!" Jinx could tell from the shocked look on Trix's face that she hadn't meant to utter a rhyme. But it was too late. As soon as the words were out of Trix's mouth the millions of shimmering purple pieces

swirled and twirled in the air as they re-formed into
the shape of the sculpture. With a final burst of
light, the sculpture magically reassembled itself and
landed back in its proper place on the shelf.

"Wow!" Oscar exclaimed.

Jinx's ears drooped. His fur was wet but an
overwhelming sense of dread was covering him too.
Now Oscar had all the proof he needed that Trix
was a witch.

Chapter Twelve

Oscar smiled his pesky younger brother smile. "Gotcha!" he told Trix and stuck out his tongue.

"What in the world is going on?" Mum shouted as she barrelled down the stairs.

"Oscar Eugene Percival Morgan!" Dad yelled as he stormed into the lounge, wearing his chef's hat and apron and carrying a bowl full of yellow batter.

Trix felt a tiny bit sorry for Oscar. He was in big trouble if Dad was already using his full name, and Oscar knew it. The smug smile faded from his face.

Then it was like watching one of those funny videos on YouTube. Mum slipped on the marbles and one lone balloon, which was still somehow balanced on the doorframe, plopped down and burst right on her head. She came crashing down on top of Trix. Jinx darted out of her way but ploughed straight into Dad who sneezed, got tangled in the

wire and also fell to the floor. The batter in the bowl exploded into the air and showered everything in the lounge.

And then Oscar made his biggest mistake – he took a picture with Mum's phone of his family piled up on the lounge floor.

"Oh, this is going to be great!" Oscar cried.

Trix could hear what sounded like a video playing on the phone. Panic flashed through her. Had he filmed her magically reassembling the sculpture?

Creeping cats!

Trix looked for Jinx. Her magical familiar was drenched with water and yellow batter. She quickly wiped him off with the hem of her shirt. "Jinx," she whispered in his ear. "I might need a little magical help."

He nodded and flicked a dollop of batter from the tip of his tail.

"You've got to see this," Oscar said as Mum and Dad struggled to their feet. He looked up from the phone and must have noticed the angry expressions on his parents' batter-splattered faces, because he backed away from them, holding up the phone like a shield. "I can explain everything."

Mum and Dad's faces glowed red. Trix had never seen her parents so angry.

"Trix is a witch!" Oscar shouted. He started tapping the screen of the phone.

"How dare you call your sister such an awful name?" Dad shouted. "Apologise to her at once!"

"Is that my phone?" Mum demanded, reaching for her mobile, but Oscar jerked it away.

"Y-yes, Mum, b-b-ut I borrowed it for a good reason," Oscar stammered.

"You borrowed it without asking," Mum said, finally snatching the phone back from Oscar.

"Please let me show you what I've filmed. You won't be angry once you know what I've discovered. We're going to be famous!" Oscar was talking fast, trying to make his parents understand.

But Trix couldn't let anyone see that video! She and Jinx crawled to Mum's side. Mum was so focused on Oscar that she didn't notice.

"*Hubble, bubble, toil and trouble,*" Trix began. She'd read that part in one of Lulu's old spell books, but she made the next part up herself. "*Erase Mum's mobile on the double.*"

Jinx wiggled and jiggled his whiskers and Trix crossed her fingers, arms, legs and toes for extra luck.

"Just look at this." Oscar grabbed the phone from Mum and called up the video, but the screen went blank. "Oh, no! What's happened? It was right here. Trix smashed that awful purple thing . . ."

"You mean your Aunt Belle's sculpture?" Dad asked and pointed to the purple sculpture on the shelf. "You mean that one, right there?"

Oscar nodded. "You have to believe me." The phone slipped from Oscar's hand. Trix stared at the phone's blank screen. She stabbed at the buttons but nothing happened. No lights. Not a flicker.

Trix's spell had worked, but it had worked too well. She seemed to have erased *everything* on Mum's phone.

"OSCAR!" her parents screamed in unison when they saw the phone lying lifeless on the floor.

Oscar darted up the stairs. "It's all Trix's fault. She *is* a witch!" he yelled over his shoulder.

"I don't know what's the matter with him," Mum said to Dad, shaking her head.

"I'm really sorry, Trix," Dad said, helping Trix up. "He shouldn't call you names."

"It's OK," Trix replied, and everything *was*

OK again. She felt a bit bad for Oscar. She really was a witch, after all. He wasn't lying about that, and he hadn't been the one to erase everything on Mum's phone.

But she only felt a *tiny* bit bad. He *had* tried to trick her. His little trap could have seriously injured someone. And he'd got away with playing loads of mean, annoying, *pesky* pranks on her in the past. But nothing changed the fact that Oscar knew Trix's secret.

From now on, Trix knew, Oscar would be like a super-scary robot, watching her with laser-like vision and programmed with only one mission – destroy Trix!

Chapter Thirteen

Trix had made it through another week of school and witchcraft lessons – but only barely. She'd had to duck and dive during Lulu's advanced tutorial on wish granting. She hadn't raised her hand once or even looked directly at Lulu. She was no closer to granting her own Wisher's wish, even though she'd been wracking her brains for a way to help Melinda.

And then there was Oscar! He'd been

following her from dawn to dusk. So far today, in order to spy on Trix, Oscar had hidden under her bed, in the kitchen cupboard and even behind the next-door neighbour's garden gnome. Now Oscar had followed Trix and Holly to the park after school and was crawling under the climbing frame to sneak up behind Trix.

"Is he still there?" Trix asked Holly.

Holly giggle-snorted. "He's trying to hide behind the swings, now. Oh!" Holly flinched. "That had to hurt. He just dived onto the moving roundabout."

"I've got to hand it to him," Trix said. "He never gives up." Trix told Holly about Oscar's Trix trap.

"Pretty smart, using chocolate – the thing you love most – against you," Holly replied, when Trix had finished her story and Holly had finished laughing at Trix's description of the scene.

"Let's try to lose him!" Trix grabbed Holly's hand and, together, the girls raced towards the edge of the park. Without warning, Trix skidded to a stop.

"Hey!" Holly said as she smacked into Trix. "What's the . . ."

"It's Melinda." Trix nodded towards Melinda, who was sitting under the tree where they'd first seen her. Her nose was stuck in a big, thick book.

Trix felt the sizzle in her brain that she always felt when a brilliant idea was cooking. "What did you say about Oscar's trap?"

Holly scrunched her eyebrows together in that *why are you asking?* way. "I said that it was smart of Oscar to use what you loved against you."

"Oh, that's it!" Trix exclaimed. "At last I have an idea for how I can get to know

Melinda better. I just need to get rid of Oscar."

Both girls glanced back. Oscar was creeping towards them on his hands and knees. When he saw them look his way, he flattened himself in the grass and closed his eyes as if he thought that might make him invisible.

Trix scanned the park in search of something to distract Oscar. She noticed a crowd gathered around the football pitch. "What's going on over there?" Trix asked, leading Holly towards the pitch.

Holly bounced up and down to see over the crowd. "It must be someone famous." *Bounce.* "Is that . . . ?" *Bounce.* "I think it might be . . ." *Bounce.* "It is!" Holly said. "It's that footballer who plays for England but used to play for that foreign team with the funny name and then was signed to that other . . ."

Strangely, Trix understood exactly who Holly meant, and this was just the distraction she needed. "Isn't that a famous footballer over there?" Trix shouted.

Holly only looked confused for a second and then she realised what Trix was doing. "Yes, that's him, right over there on the football pitch," Holly shouted extra loudly and pointed.

Oscar loved football. He immediately ran towards the football pitch. Trix and Holly high fived.

"Score!" Trix said with a laugh. "Now for the second phase of my plan . . ." Trix huddled close to Holly. "Hold out your hands." She cleared her throat. *"To make friends, you need a hook. Give us copies of Melinda's book!"*

The air swirled between them, filled with the sound of flapping pages. With a burst of light that caused both girls to squint, two copies of *The Secret Garden* plopped, one after the other, into Holly's hands.

"Oh, I love this book!" Holly squealed and hugged the copies to her chest.

"Follow my lead," Trix said, taking one of the books and tucking it under her arm. She strolled over towards Melinda. "Hi,

Melinda," Trix called when she was close enough to be heard but not so close as to scare her. When Melinda looked up from her book, Trix tried to flash the cover of her copy, as casually and naturally as she could. She had to handle this just right. "Do you mind if we join you? I'm Trix and this is Holly and we're looking for a nice place to read."

Melinda sneered. Trix hadn't seen many people actually sneer, but she thought that the expression on Melinda's face should be the image next to the dictionary definition. Trix felt the jelly babies she'd eaten earlier start a fight in her tummy. If this didn't work, Trix was absolutely out of ideas.

"Wouldn't you rather go and see that stupid famous football guy?" Melinda said and started reading again.

"No, I'd much rather talk books than football, wouldn't you, Holly?" Trix said. She had a feeling that she sounded as if she were delivering a line of really bad dialogue on a TV show.

"Yes, Trix, I especially love *this* book!" Holly said a little too enthusiastically.

Melinda didn't even look up but she said, "I suppose you can sit if you want."

Trix smiled and sat down next to Melinda. She felt the first glimmer of hope that she might accomplish her first fairy godmotherly mission after all.

Chapter Fourteen

After a little while, Trix closed her book and asked, "What's your favourite book, Melinda?"

Melinda thought for a moment. Then she said, "I like books about witches and wizards, even if I know they aren't really real. I wish they were sometimes."

Trix and Holly exchanged a look that said they were both thinking about Trix's secret.

"I believe in magic," Holly said and showed Melinda one of her best magic tricks. She reached up and pulled a coin out of thin air. She had been practising her magic and was getting really good at a few simple tricks.

"Wow!" Melinda said and her eyebrows arched in surprise.

"Holly is training to be either a world-famous magician or chef," Trix explained. "Her fairy cakes are pretty magical, too."

Silence crept in again. Melinda stared down at her book and flipped the pages. Trix and Holly looked at each other. They had to keep trying now that Melinda had opened the door of friendship a teeny tiny bit.

"Where did you live before you moved to Little Witching?" Trix asked. The girls leaned in as Melinda started talking about living in Italy and Spain, and she kept right on talking as if she'd been saving up all these things, waiting for a chance to tell someone.

"Hey, weirdos!" Oscar came charging over.

"Don't you know who that is over there?" Oscar was breathless and sweaty. "It's Simon Lloyd. He's a really, really, *really* famous footballer – even people as thick as you two should know who he is! *And* he's just moved to Little Witching!"

"Don't mind Oscar," Trix shouted over Oscar's annoying interruption. "He's just my little brother." Trix turned her back on Oscar, trying to ignore him and focus on Melinda. "It must be difficult to move house all the time. I guess books are good company."

"Books never disappoint me, but people sometimes do." Melinda stood up and dusted herself off. "I've got to go."

What had Trix done wrong?

"Hey, Mr Lloyd! Simon!" Oscar shouted, and jumped up and down excitedly.

Simon Lloyd was coming their way. He waved as he passed and Melinda half-heartedly waved back. "Glad you found some friends," he called to her. "Have fun and I'll see you at home later."

Then Trix understood. "Simon Lloyd is your dad."

As Melinda nodded, her shoulders slumped and her lips twisted into a frown.

A group of kids came rushing over to Melinda. They were all talking at once.

"You know Simon Lloyd?"

"Can you get me his autograph?"

"Do you want to come and play football with us?"

"Could your dad teach us a few tricks?"

And suddenly it all made sense. Melinda wanted to be liked for herself, not for who her father was. Trix thought it was funny how something like having a famous and talented father could be good and bad at the same time.

"Leave me alone," Melinda said, trying to push her way free of the crowd that had now surrounded her. It was no use. They kept right on following her.

"Why are you reading when you could play football?" a dark-headed boy asked, snatching Melinda's book out of her hand.

Melinda's eyes were filling with tears and her hands were clenching into fists. Trix decided it was time for a little sneaky magic. She stopped and let the crowd of kids wash around her. Oscar was right in the middle of the pack. She waited until he'd passed her.

Then Trix squeezed her eyes shut and whispered a spell ever so quietly. A few footballs came bouncing over, followed by a few more, and then a few more. Trix flicked her finger, directing the magical footballs towards the pitch and away from Melinda.

Trix lowered her voice in an effort to disguise it and called, "Free footballs to anyone who can catch one!"

A cheer erupted from the crowd as the kids turned and chased after the footballs.

"I'm so sorry about that," Trix told Melinda when everyone had gone.

"I'm used to it," Melinda said, picking up her book, which had been tossed on the ground. She didn't look like being used to it made it hurt any less.

"Maybe we could form a book club," Holly suggested. "I know a few girls in our class who like books as much as you do."

Melinda studied Trix and Holly as if they were suspects in a police line-up. "Do you really like books or are you just being nice to me to meet my dad?"

"We just want to be your friends," Trix said. "That's it."

"Really?" Melinda asked.

Trix and Holly nodded.

"Then a book club would be great!" Melinda declared. Then she added, "But absolutely no football books."

"It's a deal, Melinda!" Trix laughed.

"You can call me Lindy," Melinda told her. "That's what my real friends call me." And then Lindy smiled – a big, real, sunshine-filled smile.

Chapter Fifteen

Jinx chased a butterfly and then played tag with a squirrel. He climbed a tree. Maybe it was time for a cat nap. Jinx stretched his paws and yawned. He loved spending Saturdays in the park.

Dogs barked as they scampered after balls and frisbees. Boys and girls swarmed the football pitch like flies at a picnic. Mums pushed prams along the path. A steady stream of kids flowed like water from swings to roundabout to slide to climbing frame. Jinx thought it looked as if everyone was dancing to his or her own music.

Trix was leaning against the tree below him. Just standing there. Maybe she was thinking. Where had Holly and Lindy gone? They had come to the park with Trix, but now they seemed to have disappeared.

Meow! Jinx waved at Trix.

"Hello, Jinx Jingle Jangle!" Trix whispered.

Jinx swished his tail from side to side and crouched down, inviting Trix to play. Maybe a game of hide and seek! Meow!

"I can't play right now," Trix told him, "but maybe later. I've got something important to do first." She placed one finger to her lips. "I need you to be very quiet or you might ruin my plan."

Plan? What plan? Jinx loved a plan.

"Here he comes." Trix pointed to someone walking this way.

It was Oscar! What plan did Trix have for Oscar? He was still in trouble for his Trix trap. He kept trying to tell Mum and Dad that Trix was a witch, but that only got him into more trouble. He'd had to hoover the house, wash the dishes, weed the back garden and help Dad clear the junk out of the attic. Jinx had liked investigating the dust-covered boxes and forgotten trinkets hidden among the cobwebs. He'd found three buttons, a few coins and an old skeleton key that he was certain opened some secret attic room – although no matter how hard he looked, he couldn't find it.

Jinx's brain was swirling with thoughts. That happened to him sometimes. Concentrate, Jinx, he told himself.

"Hey, weirdo!" Oscar shouted as he stomped up to Trix. A frown was plastered on Oscar's face. "What do you want?"

Trix crooked a finger at Oscar. "Come here." Then she made a big show of making sure no one else was around. "I've got a secret to tell you."

"Why are you acting so strange?" Oscar stepped

next to Trix. "You're not going to turn me into a frog or anything, are you?"

"Don't be silly." Trix cupped her hand around her mouth and leaned over to whisper to Oscar. Jinx leaned down as far as he could without falling.

"You were right, Oscar," Trix told him. "I am a witch."

What was Trix doing? Jinx nearly fell out of the tree. He dug his claws into the bark and pulled himself back onto the branch.

Jinx jumped to the ground. He ran circles around Trix and Oscar. He had to get Trix's attention. The first rule of the Sisterhood of Magic was that she couldn't tell anyone she was a witch. She'd broken the rule once before with Holly. Lulu had asked for a special dispen-something-or-other from the Sisterhood of Magic so Holly could know, but they wouldn't like it – not one single bit – if Trix told Oscar. Holly could keep a secret, but Oscar would tell the world.

This was worse than being covered with honey in a room full of bees!

"I knew it!" Oscar shouted and punched the air.

He danced a little jig at his rightness, but then he stopped mid-wiggle. "Wait. Why are you telling me this?"

"I'm not supposed to tell anyone, but you are my little brother and I thought you should know," Trix said.

It didn't make any sense!

"Prove it!" Oscar demanded, planting his fists on his hips and glaring at his witchy sister.

"OK," Trix said and walked a few steps away from Oscar. She picked up an orange scarf that Jinx hadn't noticed lying at the base of the tree trunk. "I call upon my powers of magic. Make this scarf float away," Trix cried.

The scarf twitched in Trix's hand and then lifted up, up and away into the treetop.

But how can that be? Jinx wondered. That wasn't a rhyme. Trix hadn't cast a spell on the scarf.

"And now I will make myself disappear!" Trix shoved her hand into her pocket. "Presto chango!" she shouted and flung a handful of glitter into the air. Jinx watched the colours twinkle in the sunlight as the glitter fluttered to the ground.

Trix had vanished!

What was going on? How had Trix disappeared without casting a rhyming spell? And why was she telling Oscar her secret? Was she coming down with witching cough again – or an even more serious magical malady? Had she hit her head or had a mean witch cast a spell on her?

Jinx inspected the last place Trix had been standing. Then he whipped around to circle the tree when . . . BONK! Jinx's head hit something hard. But there was nothing there. Was it a force field? Jinx slowly stretched out a paw. The air had turned cold and hard. Had Trix's magic gone haywire?

At that moment, Oscar stepped up next to Jinx and another Oscar appeared in front of him. TWO Oscars! Double trouble!

"Nice try, weirdo!" Oscar said and knocked on the invisible force field. "Do you think I'm stupid or something? What a pathetic trick!"

Jinx looked at the two Oscars. He tapped the second Oscar, the one facing them. It wasn't a real Oscar. It was just a reflection.

It was a mirror, not magic!

Trix stepped out from behind the mirror. "I can't fool you, Oscar." Trix shook her head. A full-length mirror had been set at such an angle that, if you were standing in the right spot, it reflected the tree and grass and made it seem as if there was nothing behind the tree.

"Sorry, Trix," Lindy called from the branches above. She was holding the orange scarf and a spool of fishing wire.

"Oscar's too smart for us," Holly sighed as she carefully laid the mirror down on the grass.

Oscar frowned and then laughed. "I knew Trix

wasn't a witch. I never believed your silly tricks for a minute." Oscar kicked at the grass. "I was just pretending that I did!"

But Jinx knew that Oscar HAD believed it. It was the truth, after all.

"Girls are so stupid!" Oscar shouted, and then raced off in the direction of the football pitch.

Jinx smiled to himself. Trix wasn't stupid. She was smart! She had set her own trap for Oscar – proving him wrong by telling him he was right!

Chapter Sixteen

"**M**agically marvellous, Trix!" Lulu called as soon as Trix entered the magic classroom on Monday after school. A sparkling gem appeared on the sash that was draped across Trix's body. "You have passed your first wish-granting test!"

The other witches and familiars gathered round to congratulate Trix.

"How did you do it?" Pippa asked.

"Melinda was like a completely new person at school today. A *nice* person!"

"Did you use a Sweetness Spell?" Becka asked.

"Or was it a Non-grumpy Potion?" Cara wondered.

"Yeah, Trix," Stella said, "tell us your secret now that you've *finally* granted Melinda's wish."

Trix wouldn't let Stella's meanness upset her. Yes, it had taken a while, but she'd succeeded.

"Wish granting is not a race of speed but of kindness and imagination," Lulu said, sweeping the witches into a big hug. "And Trix is overflowing with both!"

Trix wriggled free from the hug. She *wanted* to share her secret. "In the end I didn't really have to use magic," she said. "I just needed to be kind." Trix stared at Stella and hoped she got the message.

Trix loved her new sparkly gem and she

was relieved that she'd finally succeeded in her mission, but what felt even better was knowing that she'd helped Lindy *and* found a new friend in the process.

Friendship was definitely magical!

Don't miss Trix's next exciting adventure . . .

Magic Trix

Magic Mansion
Sara Grant

Trix is desperate to attend the exciting and glamorous Sisterhood of Magic Ball, but first she must pass a series of magical tests.

Can Trix draw on all her witchy know-how – and the power of friendship – to become the belle of the ball?

Available March 2014!

the
orion star

Sign up for **the orion star**
newsletter to get inside information
about your favourite children's authors
as well as exclusive competitions and
early reading copy giveaways.

www.orionbooks.co.uk/newsletters

Follow @the_orionstar on **twitter**.

Orion
Children's Books